Some Mangled Fairy Tales

by

Mark Hayes Peacock

Cover: Mark Hayes Peacock

Contents

Little Red Hoodie

A Mangled Fairy Tale

The wolf figured he had the two youngest piglets trapped. He'd chased them into the house of the youngest, although "house" wasn't quite the best word for the little pig's dwelling, since it was made of straw. Why, a good huff and a puff and the structure would be gone.

But the wolf had done too much puffing over the years, so all he could muster was a tepid huff. He tried at a puff, but what came out was a galloping case of halitosis. That was enough, however, to disintegrate the straw, which dissolved into a pile of dust around the two piglets. Suddenly aware of their peril, the duo took off across the field to the safety of the middle piglet's house.

Once inside the stick house, which the middle pig insisted was a much stronger and safer abode than his brother's straw house, they watched as the wolf gamely limped through the front gate and came into the yard.

The wolf was exhausted. He was spent. Gasping for breath, he leaned against the piglet's front door for support. When the door gave way and fell inward, the wolf fell with it and with that the entire house fell down upon the wolf in a cascade of sticks.

By the time the wolf dug himself from the wreckage, way across another field he could see the two little pigs crossing the drawbridge over the moat surrounding the eldest pig's house. The drawbridge was pulled up after the pigs were safe inside. He picked himself up and walked slowly across the field toward the third pig's sturdy house to survey the situation.

As any younger sibling can attest, the eldest in a family always is the smartest, the most practical, the most experienced, the most intuitive, the most outgoing, the most creative, and certainly the best looking of the entire brood.

Ask any younger child if this might not be true.

And so the eldest pig had built his house of rock and cement, with six foot thick walls, heavy insulation, a moat with a drawbridge, and a front door with a slot that could open for speakeasy-style communication or, if necessary, a machine gun. What's more, the pig's home was off the grid, so no electric wires could be cut to disable the place. Water came from a well on the property and sewage had a special piping to the roof over the front door so that, when the pig opened a valve, an unwelcome visitor would receive an unwelcome shower.

The wolf considered the odds against his chances of grabbing a juicy pork dinner and just as he was deciding to throw in the towel on this attempt, he heard the sound of skipping and singing. He turned and there was Little Red Hoodie, coming down the path.

He sucked in his stomach and approached her with a smile. "Good afternoon, Missy, and it is a fine one, if I don't say so myself," he said. He suppressed a wolf whistle.

"Traviata?" he asked.

Little Red had heard smooth lines before and was quite used to them. "Yes, it is," she replied, rather than ignoring him and seeming impolite. *A wolf that knows opera? Remarkable!* It was one of the slickest pickup lines she'd ever heard. But she had grown tired of wolf whistles and pickup lines, which is why she wore her red hoodie. The less to be seen, the better, she thought.

"And where might you off to?" asked the wolf.

Little Red was not only polite, but also a bit unfiltered and had not learned yet that everything one thought need not be blurted out loud. "I'm heading over the river and through the woods to my grandmother's house," she said.

"And how is the old. . . I mean, how is your grandmother these days?"

"Oh, you know her?"

"Sure. For years," lied the wolf.

"She tweeted me this morning and said she wasn't feeling her best, so that's why I decided to visit," said Little Red. "I'm bringing her these flowers."

"Well, please tell her hello from me," said the wolf, giving Little Red a quick appraisal. A little scrawny, he thought, but after chasing fat piglets without success just about anything would satisfy his hunger. He knew a short-cut that would shave time from the path over the river and through the woods and, as he waved Red a waggly goodbye, that's the path he took.

Grandma had lived in a rural area for so long she'd never learned city habits like locking one's doors, so when the wolf arrived at her cottage, he simply walked in the back door and wolfed her down, easy as pie. Then, because he'd read somewhere that honey would alter his voice, he found some in grandma's kitchen cupboard and downed three tablespoons, after which he donned grandma's nightcap and nightgown. He closed the blinds and crawled into her bed just in time as Little Red Hoodie knocked on the front door.

"Oooh, Grandma, it's dark in here!" said Little Red. "Let me let in some light for you."

"No, please, dear; the light will hurt my eyes."

"I brought you flowers."

"How sweet of you, always thoughtful," said Grandma from inside the wolf.

"I beg your pardon?"

"Oh, just a burp," said the wolf. "Sour stomach today, my dear."

Little Red came and sat on the side of Grandma's bed. "Grandma, what pointy, hairy ears you have! I never noticed that before."

"Oh, my dear, when you get older hair grows in the oddest places: hair in your ears, hair on the end of your nose, hair on your chinny, chin, chin. Don't be surprised when it happens to you some day."

"And Grandma, what beady eyes you have!"

"The better to see you with, my dear," said the wolf, who then took a flying guess that landed well: "And I see that you are not wearing your glasses. I think your mother is right: you are too young for contact lenses, and, really, your glasses are quite attractive. You should wear them—just not right now."

"They make me look nerdy."

"Better to look nerdy than to be nerdy, I'd say."

"Your voice doesn't sound like the voice I'm used to," said Little Red.

"Late choir practice last night at church. We're rehearsing an oratorio and the choir director is working us hard. I guess I must have strained my vocal chords."

"Choir? Church choir? Why, Grandma, I didn't know you went to church."

"Oh, yes, dearie. I go to church—religiously."

"And Grandma, your breath is unpleasant today. Have you been soaking your teeth overnight, as Mother suggested?"

"Why, dearie, last night I forgot! But I promise to do better."

"Your teeth do look different, Grandma. They're so sharp looking!"

"They are sharp!" said the wolf. "The better to eat you with, my dear!" And with that he leapt out of bed. Or he would have leapt out of bed, if not for having swallowed Grandma. Three chases around Grandma's dining room table left him gasping for breath and enabled Little Red to race to the front door and fling it open. She ran smack into a man in a white smock and, close behind, the wolf met the same fate.

"What on earth?" exclaimed the wolf.

"Mobile Military recruiting station, sir" said the first man. "Allow me to introduce us. I'm Sergeant Ryan and this is Lieutenant Wigley."

"How nice of you to volunteer, sir," said the Lieutenant. "We'll begin your enlistment process with a physical exam."

"But, but, but. . . . " sputtered the wolf.

"Don't worry sir; we'll get to that part of the exam in due time," assured the Lieutenant.

He pulled a tongue depressor from a leather bag and stuck it in the wolf's mouth. "Say, aaahh," he commanded. "Aaaagh," gagged the wolf. "Help!" said Grandma. The Lieutenant raised an eyebrow. He looked over at Sergeant Ryan. "You heard that?"

"I did, sir," said Sergeant Ryan. "Split personality? Schizophrenia?"

The Lieutenant raised the other eyebrow. Sergeant Ryan checked a box on the paper form in his clipboard.

"The Lieutenant stuck a probe into each of the wolf's ears. "Lotsa wax," he pronounced. Sergeant Ryan checked a box on the paper in his clipboard.

Grandma kicked with both feet and began to use her elbows, too. The wolf grunted in pain. Grandma's thrashing round inside him really hurt. He'd never experienced such discomfort. She used her arms, legs, feet, elbows and bit the wolf wherever she could. His stomach began to heave and roll. He felt like throwing up. Sergeant Ryan made another notation on the form in his clipboard.

"Now," said the Lieutenant, "Hernia."

"That's not my name," shouted Grandma. "It's Mildred!"

The Lieutenant cocked both eyebrows. "Excuse me?" he said. Then, grabbing the wolf where things matter, he commanded, "Cough!"

The wolf coughed and out came Grandma, deposited as easily on the ground as Jonah had been spat onshore by the whale.

This time Sergeant Ryan raised both eyebrows. Lieutenant Wigley's eyebrows stood at attention. The wolf took off and Grandma and Little Red Hoodie hugged each other. "Now, I really need to go home to bed!" said Grandma.

"Not so fast," said a deep voice.

"Why, Fred! You're just in time! I've just had a most extraordinary experience!"

"A new perfume? It smells a bit like. . . . "

"Garbage?" Grandma finished.

Fred nodded. "Or at least sewer. Whatever possessed you to wear it?"

"I was just about to tell you," said Grandma. Then, turning to Little Red, she said brightly, "Dearie, please call me next week so we can arrange something. I see Fred has his backpack with him and I'd forgotten all about our tennis date this afternoon. It's a busy couple of days for us: zip lining tomorrow, then parasailing, square dancing, an excursion to an apple orchard, a golf outing and I just forget what else we have planned. Oh, white water rafting next week. I forgot! So just call me to figure out when we can get together. Oh, and this is my friend Fred."

"Pleased to meet you, Little Red," said Fred, as he took Grandma's hand.

"The flowers I brought?"

"Oh, dearie, give them to the Lieutenant. Poor thing; he looks like he could use them."

And off went Grandma and Fred.

"Well, sir," said Sergeant Ryan to Lieutenant Wigley, "So much for our monthly quota."

"Unless, young lady, you might like to consider enlisting," said the Lieutenant to Little Red. "You'd get to see some of the world and if you haven't had your fill of unwanted attention and harassment, there's a place for you with us."

Little Red declined the invitation. "What I'd like to see right now is some breakfast," she said.

"Oh," said Sergeant Ryan. "There's a nice little restaurant just down the road. It's around the curve and on the right. Looks like a cottage. They call it *Café Los Tres Osos,* which I think is Urdu for *Three Bears Cafe.* Just about everything they offer you should find to be just right."

Pulling her hoodie closed more tightly so that not a hair on her head would be visible, Little Red Hoodie started down the road. Turning, over her shoulder she said, "Thank you for the tip. I do hope they serve porridge."

The cafe did look like a cottage and Little Red seated herself on a stool at the counter. She loosened her hoodie and let a profusion of blonde curls cascade to her shoulders.

"And what can I get you this morning?" asked the hefty waitress, as she righted an upturned white cup and poured in coffee without being asked for it.

"Do you serve porridge?"

"We do!" answered the waitress. Slipping her hand to the side of her mouth as if she were sharing a secret, she added: "Porridge is a house specialty. It's made by our owner and it's delicious!"

"Then, porridge. And some orange juice, an egg over easy and an English muffin."

With a jolly "coming up!" the waitress disappeared behind a swinging door to the kitchen.

"You'll want to make sure you put paprika or curry or chili pepper sauce on those eggs," said a man with a moustache, black hair that looked like axle grease had slicked it back, gold chains highlighting a well-tanned chest and a shirt cut to here. He slid onto the stool next to Little Red. "You don't want bland eggs. You need to give eggs some spice, some real heat, to make eating them worthwhile."

"You know about those things, I take it?" said Little Red.

"Baby, I know about those things for sure! I also know there's a good band tonight at a bar this side of the river. I could see that you'd have a hot time."

"I don't think so," said Little Red. "And right now I need a bit of peace and quiet, so I'm going to ask you nicely to move away."

"Babe, you don't know what you'll be missing. You look hot to me; I like hot."

"Well then, you need to cool it," said Little Red.

Just then the hefty waitress reappeared. She stood across from Little Red with her arms folded, glaring at the man with the moustache. He seemed to shrink in size as he slid off the stool. Then, recovering, he headed out the door, walking with a backward tilt as his head and feet seemed to follow his torso.

"Too hot," said Little Red to the waitress.

The waitress nodded and then inclined her head to the other end of the counter where a skinny man sat staring at his phone. He wore a pinstriped blue suit, a blue tie, and white shirt. "More coffee, Sid?" she said.

The man grunted and didn't look up from his phone. The waitress poured him a refill anyway. The man ignored the courtesy.

"Too cold," said Little Red to the waitress, who then disappeared into the kitchen, reappearing quickly with Little Red's porridge.

Little Red dipped a spoon into the bowl of porridge. She tasted. "Mmmmm," she said to the waitress. "This is just right! My compliments to the chef."

"I'll call him," said the waitress. "You can tell him yourself."

Soon the waitress reappeared, towing an embarrassed young man behind her. He was tall and lanky, built like an upside down triangle, and had an "Aw shucks!" manner. Porridge specks decorated his white apron.

"You like our porridge?" he asked.

"It's delicious! Just right!"

"We try," he said. "People do tell us it is very good. We serve a lot of it."

"You must have a special recipe."

"It's my late mother's. She had the place until I took it over."

The hefty waitress disappeared discretely into the kitchen. Little Red looked around. The café was decorated brightly with white tables and armchairs, several booths along one wall and more along the window wall on the street side. Strung along the back wall was a bear hide next to the head of a ten point buck.

"Your mother's trophies?" asked Little Red.

"Mine," said the chef. "Some people don't like them, but I'd like to add a few more."

"Like?"

"I'd like to have a wolf's skin hanging there, too."

Little Red thought for a moment. This all seemed just right. The café owner seemed just right. His porridge certainly was just right. She could see just the right place for a wolf's hide on the back wall.

She turned to face the chef. "I hear there's a good band tonight at the bar by the river" she said. "Would you like to go?"

Jack and the Bean Sprouts

Another Mangled Fairy Tale

By

Mark Hayes Peacock

Mom had gone vegan so the cow had to go. "Bring it to the village," she said to her son Jack. "Get the most you can for it."

Getting rid of the cow made Jack sad, for he was an only child and he and the cow had been best friends, gamboling in the yard together and having great conversations. Jack was sure that the cow laughed when he tossed a cow pie and that the cow nodded approval when he sailed one for more yardage than any tossed before. The cow had trotted beside Jack as he paced off the distances and marked them. When Jack took an old red towel and played "bull fighter", the cow tolerantly played along, charging at Jack and then veering off so as not to snag her horns in the towel.

The cow and Jack were quite a pair. The cow was just what Jack needed as an only child with a widowed mother.

Disconsolate about having to take his friend to town, Jack trudged toward the village, leading the cow by an old dog leash. They passed a field with high grass in need of mowing. At the driveway of the property there was a produce stand manned by a spry, skinny man.

"It's a hot day," said the man. "I can give you a glass of water."

Jack thought that was a good idea and after he took several sips, shared his water with the cow.

"Where 'ya headed?" asked the man.

"To the village. Mom says we need to sell the cow. She's gone vegan; milk and meat aren't allowed."

The man thought for a moment. "A cow could do some good around here," he said. "In fact, a cow could be the making of good things here." He swept his arm toward the overgrown grass field. "Turn her loose for some months here and then I can say she's organic. Organic milk costs plenty. My markup potential is super! I can price it outrageously! Why, in a short time I can be rich!" He faced Jack. "How much for the cow?"

Jack looked blank. He had no idea.

"Tell you what," said the man. "I have some great bean sprouts right here." He reached into a basket on the counter of his stand and grabbed a handful. "These are special!"

Jack was paying close attention. "Why, these sprouts will enhance your growth so you reach your potential height. Now, wouldn't that be nice?"

Jack nodded.

"What's more, these special sprouts will make you smart—smarter even than the smartest girl in your class! Guaranteed! They'll also make you wise, way beyond your years, so you don't have to learn life's lessons the hard way—by experience. They also have the power to make you rich, rich beyond your greatest imagination. Why, your mother will be so proud of you!"

He placed the sprouts in a paper bag with a careful flourish. Then, looking at Jack intently, he said, "'Course what I just said has not been approved by the Food and Drug Administration, but it's all true. You can check it out on the Internet and you'll see it's all true."

Jack took the bag of sprouts and traded it for the cow's leash. After giving the cow a hug, he turned toward home.

Jack's mother hit the roof of course when he returned home with no money and a bag of bean sprouts. Angrily, she threw them into a large bowl of lettuce, tomatoes, cucumbers and red peppers. "There aren't even enough left over for a sandwich for tomorrow's lunch!" she said. Then she burst into tears.

They ate dressing-less salad in silence. Jack vowed to make it up to his mother, how he did not know, but he figured he owed her.

After a solid night's sleep Jack awoke to an amazing racket. Right outside his yard there were machines at work and men scrambling all over the place. A large sign spelled out "P.O.T.U.S. Tower" with a subtitle: "Greatness is at hand!" The noise continued all day. Without his cow companion, Jack was a bit at loose ends for what to do, a bit like when summer vacation starts to get old but one would never confess that getting back to school might be a good thing and at least it would fill out the day.

The men went home precisely at 5:01 p.m. and then there was quiet. Jack ventured beyond his fence to inspect the machinery. There was a cherry picker amid the tractors, bulldozers and backhoes. Jack had seen a tree trimmer work a cherry picker once and it seemed easy enough. He climbed into the bucket and jiggled the handles. Suddenly, the bucket rose and kept rising.

When it came to a stop, Jack found himself in a large plaza. Ahead of him was a large grey house, almost a castle, or at least it could have been a castle if one squinted a bit. The front door stood ajar

and Jack ventured through it. As he moved quietly down a long hall, he

heard a deep and threatening voice:

Fee, fi,fo, fum!

Fee, fi, fiddle-I, oh, oh, oh, oh,

Fee, fi, fiddle-I, oh,

Strummin' on the old banjo!

Jack peeked around the corner. There, seated with a gold banjo

the size of a truck tire, was a huge man, a giant of a man with his eyes

closed, picking and singing and grinning. "*Musta eaten lots of those

special bean sprouts,*" thought Jack.

He ventured further down the hall. Through an open door to his

right he could see an extraordinarily ugly woman working at a stove.

On a platter on the counter next to her lay two enormous steaks, the

largest Jack had ever seen. He moved slowly and quietly, hoping not to

be noticed by the huge man or the woman in the kitchen. He passed

through an open door into a small yard next to the kitchen and suddenly

found himself being followed by a large chicken. The chicken was

gold, which Jack thought an odd color for a chicken, for all the

chickens he'd known were either brown or white. He couldn't figure

out why a chicken would follow him; as far as he knew, only geese imprinted and followed people. Maybe it's because I'm different and it's not used to people like me, he thought.

The chicken ran ahead of Jack a bit and Jack followed. It led him to a nest beneath a corner of the back stairs and in the nest Jack found a large golden egg. He picked it up. The chicken kept brushing up against Jack's leg, so he picked it up too and returned to the long hallway he'd come through before. Tiptoeing, Jack retraced his steps and somehow, he didn't know how, restrained himself from joining in on the chorus of "Strummin on the old banjo" as he passed the front room.

Suddenly, there was a shout: "Fee! Fie, Fo!!" and the sound of large feet pounding down the hall from the kitchen. The woman in the kitchen shouted to the giant, "My chicken is missing! There must be a hole in the fence! Quick! Go out in front to see if you can catch her!"

Jack heard the twang as the giant put down his banjo and began to head toward the hall. Clutching the golden chicken under one arm and holding the golden egg in his other hand, he raced for the cherry picker, jumped into the bucket, nudged a lever with his elbow, and started back down to the ground.

Safe on the ground, Jack raced into the house. "Look, mother, see what I found!" he shouted, even as he hoped she would not be as upset as she was when he came home with the bean sprouts.

Mother appraised Jack's find with shrewd consideration. "Those are a good find, Jack," she said. "We can keep them but we need to make sure they are safe. The egg especially will come in handy when the currency devalues—which it is sure to do, soon enough."

And so they kept the golden chicken and its egg. Jack made a nest for the chicken under his bed. Even though it was not as good a companion as the cow had been, the chicken did follow him around and was company enough.

Some days passed but Jack couldn't help but think about the castle and its giant. At last he couldn't stand it any longer, so he decided to return to the castle.

By this time the workers had completed enough of the tall building that it had a working elevator. When the workers knocked off for the day, Jack vaulted his back fence, found the elevator and pressed the button labeled "Penthouse Suite". When the doors opened, instead of a lavish apartment Jack saw the familiar grey house at the end of a long walkway. Again, the front door was open and Jack snuck in.

Right away, Jack heard the same song:

Fee, fi, fo, fum!

Fee, fi, fiddle-I-oh, oh,

Fee, fi, fiddle-I-oh,

Struummin' on the old banjo!

Jack peeked around the corner and saw the giant there with his eyes closed, picking and grinning as he plucked away at his golden instrument. Jack ventured further along the hallway and looked into the kitchen. Again on the counter, he saw two huge steaks, these even larger than those he'd seen before.

"No need to go further," thought Jack. *"This is good enough!"*

He grabbed the steak platter and took off down the hallway, trying to ignore the droplets of grease that fell from the platter to betray his path. And, sure enough, he heard the ugly woman's scream when she found her steaks missing from the counter.

"The dog! The dog!" she screamed. "Quick, run to the front door and catch the dog! It took our dinner!"

Jack ran as fast as he could and got into the elevator just as the giant reached his front door. Did the giant see him? Jack could only wonder.

"Look, mother," he called as he came into the house. "Look what I brought!"

Jack was not really sure about his mother's reaction to bringing meat into a vegan household. Would she be angry with him again?

"Oh, a respite!" said mother. "Backsliding can be forgiven. For weeks now I've been longing for a nice, juicy steak!" And she lit the broiler, got out her sharpest knives and set the table for two.

The steaks were good—very good—and there were enough of the tender filets for another meal and lunch the next day, too.

However, Jack couldn't help but think about a return to the castle, sooner rather than later. And sooner was when Jack made it happen. Again, when the workers had gone home for the day, Jack took the elevator to the Penthouse Suite floor and again when the elevator doors opened he found the walkway that led to the grey castle. Again, the front door stood ajar and again he tiptoed into the hallway.

Today, however, there was no singing, picking and grinning. Instead, there was the sound of a chainsaw. Jack peeked around the corner and saw the giant asleep. The chainsaw sound was the giant's snoring. And next to the giant was the golden banjo. Tiptoeing carefully, Jack picked up the banjo and began moving toward the hallway.

Suddenly, the banjo began to play. All by itself, it plucked out the tune the giant had seemed to play when he sang along.

The giant awoke to the sound of his playing banjo. Seeing Jack he rose and began pursuit. His huge strides covered plenty of ground and Jack ran as fast as he could, burdened by the heavy golden banjo. He reached the elevator and jabbed the "down" button. Helplessly, he watched the numbers as the elevator slowly ascended to the Penthouse Suite. He dared not look back, but squeezed into the elevator the minute the doors parted. The doors closed and Jack heard the giant slam into the just-closed elevator doors. There was a dull thud; Jack hoped it was the sound of the giant falling to the ground, knocked out cold.

Mother didn't know quite what to do with a golden banjo, but Jack did. He learned to play a number of tunes, or, rather he taught the banjo to play a number of tunes, and billed himself as "Jack The Riffer". He became quite famous, to say nothing of becoming quite rich, and his world tours were sell-outs in all the major cities. When their little house was acquired for a parking lot by the P.O.T.U.S Towers, Jack bought his mother a large suite in the Towers. She could enjoy a spectacular view from there and from the window both of them could see the strip mall where the produce stand once stood.

Jack got letters from the cow once in awhile, mailed from her estate in Santa Barbara, California. Her very rich organic milk had made her and the skinny man very wealthy indeed and they'd hit the jackpot and had become even richer when the strip mall developers bought the pasture and the produce stand. She and the skinny man came to one of Jack's concerts and she nodded approval, much as she used to nod approval when judging Jack's cow pie tosses.

Eventually, Mom tired of the vegan life and ate the chicken.

The golden egg? It resided in a shoe box under Mom's bed, ensconced and carefully cushioned amid stacks of recipe cards.

She kept the egg there—just in case.

The Many Trials

A Mangled Fairy Tale
by

Mark Hayes Peacock

"Better take a number," muttered the young man to Horatio as Horatio watched

him shoehorn his way into his gray Jaguar convertible. Horatio turned

around. There was a line, alright, but the young men exiting the castle

with their heads down were more numerous than those going into the

castle.

"Please fill out the form and then read and sign the second

form," directed the clerk, as he handed Horatio papers and a pen. "The

signature is required to make sure you understand the agreement."

Horatio read. Things seemed pretty straightforward: there

would be a series of tests for any young man desiring to marry the

princess. Fail any of the tests and you'd lose your head.

What had been a line quickly disappeared and Horatio found himself alone in the presence of the king.

"I see you have left blank the make, model and license of your automobile," said the king.

"I came by bicycle."

"Bicycle? What are you, a tree hugger? Or can't you afford a car?"

"A car's expensive."

"So you have no money?"

"When I marry your daughter, my financial status won't be an issue then, will it?"

The king looked at Horatio over his cheaters and said nothing. He saw a tall, slim young man wit a determined look who, unlike many in the kingdom, seemed unafraid to look at him directly.

"You do understand the agreement you signed?"

"I do," said Horatio.

"I need to say that we must proceed according to tradition. Trials to win the hand of a princess are a long and storied tradition. And, after all, if it were not for tradition, there wouldn't be kings, queens, and princesses. Are you ready for the trials?"

"First, I'd like to meet your daughter."

"That can be arranged." The king picked up a nearby telephone and called for the princess. "Better relax," he said to Horatio. "Assuming you do pass the tests, you'll spend the rest of your life waiting for women, so you'd better get used to it." The king closed his eyes and quickly nodded off.

Horatio took the opportunity to look around at his surroundings, which certainly were grand, as befitted a castle. He'd crossed the moat on his way in and passed through the pair of guards at the entry gate, who stood at parade rest with their lances tipped slightly and their free hands placed correctly behind their chain-mailed torsos. The reception room in which he sat was magnificent: heavy red velvet draperies flanked the floor to ceiling windows, fine wooden chests adorned with inlaid gold graced each wall, the king's mahogany desk boasted a burgundy leather top, and his throne had gilt arms and back with the finest of green silk cushioning. The chandeliers glittered as crystal prisms refracted the light into sparkles throughout the room. It was a nice setting indeed, and Horatio thought he could get used to it.

His observations were interrupted by the scent of an exotic perfume. The king's eyes popped open at the same time as Horatio arose to his feet. He stood looking at the most beautiful human being he'd ever seen. Her figure was worthy of a men's magazine. Her blue eyes focused on his and seemed to drill shafts through him. Her dark hair fell gently across her shoulders and her sudden smile almost knocked him backwards. Suddenly, his sensibilities were doing cartwheels somewhere out beyond the castle moat and his tongue had outgrown his mouth.

The princes glanced at the paperwork on her father's desk. "You are Horatio?" she asked in a voice that made the world's most melodic music sound like barnyard noise.

"Yes," Horatio managed to stammer.

She extended her hand. He took it. It was the softest touch he'd ever experienced.

"I'm pleased to meet you," she said.

Horatio's legs felt like rubber. He thought he might dissolve into a puddle on the floor.

The king observed the couple's lengthy hand-hold and cleared his throat. "We need to talk about the trials," he said. "There will be three. It's tradition. You understand: you must pass each test or. . . . "

"Yes, I understand," said Horatio.

"Well then, let's proceed. Come with me. You will have to let go of each other. My dear, Horatio and I will go down to the barnyard."

With a lingering glance backwards, Horatio dutifully followed the king down rock-walled, torch lit circular stairways and then more circular stairways until they came to an outer door. The king led the way to a pile of watermelons in a corner of the pig pen.

"We recycle here," said the king. "These watermelons are a bit overripe, unfit to serve royal guests. But we need the seeds for next year's crop. Your challenge: separate the rinds for recycling and the seeds for planting. The seeds will go in the trash can there. And there will be no mess: you eat the watermelons. Overripe, yes, but they're still tasty. There's a knife. Oh, and the deadline is sunrise tomorrow morning." With that, the king turned on his heel and left.

Horatio selected a large melon to use as a seat and thought. Idly, he sliced a watermelon and tossed the pink meat to a nearby pig. The pig quickly gobbled up the juicy fruit. It was a large pig, pink itself, with a curly tail. When Horatio was a child, he used to play a game with his dog and cat, pretending to pull at their whiskers. The pig had a curly tail. It was begging TO BE PULLED STRAIGHT.

The pig let out a squeal and a mouthful of watermelon seeds rocketed toward the trash can. It took Horatio but a moment to take off the trash can lid and prop it on the edge of the barnyard fence atop the can. If he'd had paint, it could have been a target. He quartered another watermelon and set it in front of the pig.

*   *   *   *   *   *

The smell of perfume and the shadow of the king roused Horatio from his slumber. The sun peeked over the edge of the castle. In the corner of the barnyard watermelon rinds were stacked neatly. The trash can was filled to the brim with watermelon seeds.

"Um-humm," said the king. "An antacid?"

"No need," said Horatio.

"Well, I need one," said the king. "Whatever was going on down here, the racket kept me awake most of the night. Lots of squealing and honking noises."

The princess flashed Horatio a thumbs up.

"Another trial?" asked Horatio.

"Another trial. It's tradition," said the king. "This one is a different sort of challenge. By the end of the royal banquet tomorrow night you must bring me something that is both hot and cold at the same time."

"That sounds like a worthy challenge."

"Oh, I've thought about it for along time. Nothing's too good for my little girl," said the king as he put an arm around her shoulder. *I wish that were my arm*, thought Horatio.

Horatio found a corner to be by himself for most of the day. The sun was beginning to set as the banquet guests started to arrive. They swept into the royal dining room, leaving their chauffeurs and footmen outside to tend to their limousines and carriages. *It seems to be tradition, too,* thought Horatio, as he heard each guest announced, for there to be royal titles for people who no longer had kingdoms. He headed toward the kitchen.

It was a sumptuous banquet in the enormous castle dining room, its long mahogany table lit by tapers in the largest of silver candlesticks and set with elegant silverware, white linen napkins and the best of European china. The meal itself featured the finest cuts of roast beef and lamb, vegetables *al dente*, good wine, *escargot* and appetizers, and salad with the castle specialty dressing.

All that remained was coffee and dessert. The dessert herald blew a blast on his trumpet and the dessert procession began. In came the wait staff with Horatio at its head, each bearing a white bowl. Horatio set his bowl in front of the king.

"What's this?"

"Something hot and cold at the same time, your majesty."

The king regarded his bowl for several moments. Tentatively, he took his spoon and tried a bite.

"And what is it?" he asked.

"A hot fudge sundae," replied Horatio. "Hot and cold at the same time, just as you asked."

"Well, it's delicious!" declared the king. Everyone applauded and immediately dug into their bowls of hot fudge sundae. The princess signaled Horatio two thumbs up.

When they had finished, the king rose to his feet. "This young man has done well," he said. "But there is one more test. This one, the last, will be the most difficult. That, too, is what tradition demands. You all might as well hear it; he returns—and that is, if he returns from this quest—he may very well not keep his head, so everyone needs to know why. You, Horatio, must bring me the Golden Fleece. You have a full year, 365 days, in which to return here with the Golden Fleece."

"The Golden Fleece? You mean, as in Jason?"

"As in Jason."

"That's legend, not real."

"The Golden Fleece."

*   *   *   *   *   *   *

Horatio wheeled his bicycle across the castle drawbridge. He looked back wistfully and could see the princess watching from her bedroom window. He had a year, but how to find an object known only in mythology?

"This is the Gold Coast, alright," said the real estate agent in Spain. "But there's no Golden Fleece around here. I do have a condo I could sell you cheap. We're a bit overbuilt just now so real estate here is a bargain."

The princess sent Horatio a selfie of herself with her pony.

*   *   *   *   *   *   *

"A Golden Fleece here? Not on your life!" said the goo-covered roustabout. "Here in North Dakota we call this "black gold" but there's no Golden Fleece. I think there's a sheep farm over near Minot. Oh, and the employment office is out in Williston."

The princess sent Horatio a selfie of herself in her Porsche convertible.

*   *   *   *   *   *   *

"A Golden Fleece?" said the teacher in Minnesota. "We used to have gold stars, but not anymore, not since every child is special. You don't want anyone to think that someone is better than anyone else. But a fleece that's gold? Not to my knowledge."

The princess sent Horatio a selfie of herself kissing her parakeet. *I wish I were that bird right now*, thought Horatio and he pressed on to another possible site.

*   *   *   *   *   *   *

There's gold ion them thar hills!" shouted the grizzled geezer in Placerville, California. "It's just waiting there for you to find it. But no Golden Fleece that I've ever heard of around here. I do have a map you can buy. I got it from an old miner who'd found the Mother Lode but then was murdered. You're young and strong; you could be rich!"

"I'll pass," said Horatio. "I'll keep looking. But thanks."

The princess sent Horatio a selfie of herself clowning with her girl friends.

*   *   *   *   *   *   *

"There's plenty of gold locked up here, but no fleece," said the guard at Fort Knox, Kentucky. "And, sir, you'll have to step back from that line."

This was becoming discouraging.

The princess sent Horatio a selfie of herself with her foot on a watermelon.

*   *   *   *   *   *   *

"They're golden alright," said the man on a ladder in Washington State. "We call them Golden Delicious. And they are delicious. Here, have a bite." He handed Horatio an apple. Horatio bit. It was delicious. "But as for that Golden Fleece thing, I don't know," continued the man. "Wasn't that some sort of legend, something that was never really real? Either way, I wish you luck. You can have the rest of that apple."

The princess sent Horatio a selfie of herself at the zoo, wearing a feather boa, standing in front of the python's glass cage as she offered the camera an apple.

* * * * * * *

"Oh, there's plenty of gold down there," said the foreman of a mine in South Africa. "It's tough work in tough conditions and we're always looking for good workers. The pay isn't much, but it's a living of sorts. You'll find gold but you won't find a Golden Fleece here."

Horatio declined the job offer.

The princess sent Horatio a selfie of herself in a bikini. *If I could only blow that up into a poster*, thought Horatio, but then he thought of the soft hand she'd extended to him and decided her presence was better.

* * * * * * *

"It's our job to keep this bridge as shiny as gold," said the painter as he hung in a bucket over the edge of the Golden Gate Bridge. "We want to keep the image of a golden bridge, and, besides, the pay is good. Sorry, though; our roster is full so there are no jobs available. If you do find a Golden Fleece, spray paint will be easier to handle than a brush to keep it shiny."

The princess sent Horatio a selfie of herself jumping her horse over a high fence.

*   *   *   *   *   *   *

"There was gold alright," said the tour guide at the dock in London. "This is a replica of the Golden Hind that circumnavigated the world and came back with a boat load of Spanish gold for Queen Elizabeth. Sir Francis Drake, the Hind's captain, was knighted for that. But there was no Golden Fleece. I'm sorry, young man."

The princess sent Horatio a selfie of herself curled up on a sofa reading a book. *I'd like to be curled up there just now, too*, thought Horatio. This trial was getting to be more than tedious.

*   *   *   *   *   *   *

"We have plenty of gold, but they're gold medals," said the man from the International Olympics Committee in Lausanne, Switzerland. "No Golden Fleece, though. Never even heard of it. But which event do you want to compete in? Pole vaulting? Ski jumping? For pairs ice skating, you'll need a partner. And, of course, you'll have to qualify locally in order to compete in the Olympics. Downhill slalom, maybe?"

"Maybe later," said Horatio. He thought that if he pair skated with the princess, he would learn to skate and train, train and practice as hard as he could.

The princess sent Horatio a selfie of herself building a snowman.

*   *   *   *   *   *   *

"All that glitters is not gold," intoned the guru in front of his cave at the foot of the mountains in Kashmir. "The Golden Fleece is a Western myth and you know it. Young man, Krishna says you're in trouble."

The princes sent Horatio a selfie of herself in a sweeping gown that was taken at a royal ball. "Time is running out," she tweeted. "You've been gone almost a full year."

*   *   *   *   *   *   *

"Well, they're gold alright," said the plantation owner in Guatemala. "But they're bananas and when they ripen, of course they turn yellow. But there's no fleece here. There is a sheep *finca*, a ranch just across the border. You might try there. See if they have a sheep that's not white."

*   *   *   *   *   *   *

The king flipped over the hourglass and then consulted his Rolex. "Time's just about up," he said.

"Yes," sighed the princess. "Tomorrow's a full year."

Suddenly, there was a trumpet blast. "Sire, the young man, Horatio!" announced the herald as Horatio strode into the reception room. The princess restrained herself but gave Horatio a long look. He was sunburned and a bit ruffled looking with bumps and bites here and there, but otherwise not much worse for wear. As for Horatio, seeing the princess in person was far better than any selfie. Their gazes lingered.

"The quest?" interjected the king.

Horatio handed the king a pelt.

"What? This is just an ordinary sheepskin!" said the king. "You were to bring back the Golden Fleece or lose your head. Where is the Golden Fleece?"

"You have it—or them," said Horatio, as he scratched himself. The princess began to scratch herself, too and then so did the king.

"What kind of pests did you bring in here?" demanded the king.

"Look carefully, your majesty. They jump quickly."

The king grabbed a hopping insect between his thumb and finger.

"As you can see, your majesty, those fleas are gold. I found them in Chiriqui, in Panama."

"Golden fleas?"

"You didn't use spellcheck, your highness. Golden fleas they are. Do I keep my head?"

Over the tops of his cheaters the king looked at Horatio. "You do have a good head about you. You can keep it. But please get rid of the fleas."

The princess applauded and than ran to fling her arms around Horatio.

*   *   *   *   *   *   *

After the palace was fumigated, the princess and Horatio were married. It as a gala wedding, with all the glamour a traditional kingdom could muster. Horatio and his princess then set about the business of living happily ever after. They gave to the poor all but one of their wedding gift toasters and donated four of their new crystal punch bowls to the local meal site.

In due time, the princess gave birth to a prince. There was much rejoicing throughout the kingdom but not as much rejoicing for Horatio, who couldn't sleep when the infant prince didn't sleep through the night.

Late one night, when the princess was nursing the heir to the throne, instead of tossing in bed and trying to get back to sleep, Horatio spent his awake time exploring parts of the castle he'd not seen before. He went down one corridor and then up another. Returning to their quarters, he said to the princess, "What's with the large bedroom piled from floor to ceiling with mattresses? I mean, there are inflatable mattresses, pillowtop mattresses, form-remembering mattresses, innerspring mattresses, all piled on top of each other from floor to ceiling. What's the story? Why all the mattresses?"

The princess looked down adoringly at her baby prince, cradled in her arms and now sleeping soundly. She smiled. All too soon he would be grown, a young prince in search of the right woman to marry.

"Tradition," she said.

Sinner Ella

Another Mangled Fairy Tale
by

Mark Hayes Peacock

Ella was fed up with Weeping Willow By The Babbling Brook Community Church. She was tired of being told how to think and for whom to vote. She was tired of Pastor Bud, with his razor sculpted hair that made him two inches taller at least and his $2,400 silk suits and French cuffs with lots of linen showing and his patent leather shoes. She was tired of being distracted by the television camera's roving boom and of seeing Pastor Bud on a large screen when he was preaching at the other campus some Sundays. She was tired of slick music by highly paid professional musicians mostly singing about themselves when Ella thought they should be praising God. Although the music was done excellently, it just didn't relate to her.

She decided to find somewhere else to worship, which was why one Sunday she skipped breakfast and ended up in a different part of town. Hearing the thumping of a heavy bass line and the pounding of drums that came from a tall brick building with arched windows and a shiny steeple, she decided to check out what was going on inside.

"You're in luck," intoned the white-gloved usher as he handed Ella a bulletin. "We have the praise band playing this morning!"

Ella found a seat.

"He has made me glad, yes, He has made me glad,

I will rejoice for He has made me glad!"

warbled the praise band as its members stood rigidly with their hands at their sides unless they strummed or beat an instrument. It was the most solemn "praise band" Ella had ever seen and they sure didn't look glad.

Suddenly, there was a woman at Ella's left side. "You're in my place," she said. Ella processed this for a moment and then decided to slide further down the same row. Even more startling to Ella was a man in a white dress who appeared suddenly as the Praise Band ended its warbling. He mumbled several announcements and then, climbing a steep staircase to a lofty perch above the congregation, peering down at the assemblage and half-hidden behind a large wooden eagle, he began to speak on **"The Significance Of The Begats In The Development Of Nineteenth Century Western European Theology"**.

What on earth IS a 'begat'? Ella wondered.

The *begats* went on for some time. Ella was aware of soft snoring from somewhere behind her. She looked around. The arched windows were quite pretty, with stained glass depictions of men with long hair in robes doing things like holding lambs or pouring water on the head of someone else. She was impressed with the array of silver pipes along one wall, some longer than others. She thought they might be pipes for an organ.

The man in the white dress followed the *begats* with more announcements that Ella could not understand and, suddenly, a brass plate was coming down the row in her direction. Ella realized suddenly that she'd had no breakfast. *Oh, good! Some snacks!* she thought. But when the brass plate landed in front of her there were no snacks, just cash. "Well, that's very thoughtful," she said to herself and took a twenty from the plate before passing it to the lady on her left.

Ella liked the church aerobics, too. Stand, sit, kneel, stand, sit again, kneel again. *This must be a healthy congregation*, she thought. *I just wish I'd had breakfast; I'm starving!*

Very quickly afterwards Ella found people forming two lines from her seat to the front. She joined one and as she got near the head of her line she saw that, at last, there were snacks, or at least bread without butter. The man in the white dress held out a loaf of bread to her. Ella copied what she'd seen people do and pulled off a large hunk of bread to eat. She had no time to chew the mouthful of bread before a fat woman dressed in black extended a silver cup in her direction. *I hope there's enough to wash down this bread,* she thought and took a deep drink. What she got wasn't quite enough so she took another deep swallow. That was better! And yet just across the aisle there was more bread. With no snacks passed down her row and nothing but cash Ella still felt hungry, so she crossed the aisle and pulled off another hunk of bread. The man just ahead of her had dipped his bread into the wine, so Ella copied him, thinking that she might not have to wash down her bread if it were a bit moist. She dipped her bread into the wine. Promptly, the bread disintegrated.

Crumbs and bits of bread floating around in the wine would never do. Ella had to retrieve her bread; it had caused such a mess. She reached into the wine and grabbed the largest hunk of bread. Fishing around, she managed to gather several more pieces. Now, her hand was dripping wine but, fortunately, the fat woman in black had a small napkin. Ella took it and, cradling the soggy dripping bread in the napkin in her hand, returned to her seat.

The service finished with a blast from the large pipe organ and Ella followed the rest of the crowd to a large room in the back. Here— at last—was real food! Ella piled her plate high and also managed to balance a cup of weak and oily coffee. She found a place to sit and because no one bothered her she was able to enjoy a real meal in peace.

When she finished, she took her dirty plate, cup and silverware to the kitchen.

"That's as far as you go!" declared a waspish gray haired woman. "This is MY kitchen; no one else is allowed in!"

"I was going to do my dishes," said Ella. "I'm used to it; I do all the dishes and cleaning at home."

"Well, you don't get to do that here," said the woman. "This is my turf! If I let anyone else in here, everything goes haywire. People don't put things in the right place; the grill doesn't get cleaned; sometimes people take things home and don't bring them back; it's just terrible!" She took Ella's plate, cup and silverware.

I would think that a kitchen in a church building would be owned by everyone, not just one person, thought Ella. *Oh well, I might as well go home; there will be plenty of dishes to do there.*

And dishes to do was just what Ella found when she returned home. Her stepmother had left a list of chores to be done before she and Ella's stepsisters returned from her girls' cheerleading practice. In addition to the dishes, the list included washing the kitchen floor, cleaning the toilets, changing the bed linens and a few more things Ella knew she'd never get around to doing in time.

She heard muttering in the living room and in response found a large bowl and filled it with potato chips. She brought it to the living room and placed it on the table in front of her father, whose attention was focused on a televised football game. Taking an empty bowl from the table, she said, "I take it they're losing again?" Her father grunted and then growled as a fullback was thrown for a large loss. Ella returned to the kitchen. She knew that was about as far as she would get for attention from her father, who went AWOL when he married a woman with two daughters. Back when he used to talk with Ella he explained the daughters' names: "Madison and Portland were taken and Mother insisted on being creative and on keeping up with the times, so she named her girls Detroit and Atlanta."

Cheerleading was a possibility for Ella's stepsisters, as they were too chunky for ballet and too slow and too short for volleyball or basketball. Charm school might have helped them, but there was no such thing in Ella's town and Ella was sure they would have been slow learners anyway.

Ella managed to get the dishes done, the kitchen floor washed and the toilets cleaned before her stepmother and stepsisters returned. The two girls ignored Ella and went upstairs immediately, arguing as they went about whose socks were the yellow ones. Ella received the expected bawling out from her stepmother for the items on the list left undone and no praise at all for what had been done.

Trying to be pleasant, Ella told her stepmother about her church experience. "You clueless idiot!" her stepmother exploded. "You're supposed to put money INTO the plate, not take it out!"

Ella was grateful that her stepmother didn't seize the twenty.

Taking cash from the collection plate had been a blunder for sure, and it began to work on Ella. She felt great guilt. How could she have been so stupid? She determined to make things right.

It took awhile for Ella to find the church again, but she recognized the shiny steeple easily when she got to the other part of town. The large front doors were locked but she found an open side door and tiptoed in. There was light at the end of a hall and she soon found herself in the church kitchen. A young man there was mopping the floor. He looked up and saw Ella.

"I don't know how on earth people get clean floors with this," he said. "All I do is swirl mud around. Nothing comes clean."

"Here," said Ella. "I'll show you."

She took the mop from the young man and wrung it out well. Frequent rinsing and wringing soon produced a clean floor.

"I'm impressed!" said the young man. "How did you learn to do that?"

"Lots of practice," said Ella.

"It's lunch time," said the young man. "Join me?"

"That depends on what you're serving."

"Mac and cheese. I think there's enough in the box for two—if you're not too hungry."

Ella and the young man suddenly became aware that the waspish woman of the kitchen had been standing in the doorway.

"Hi there, Mrs. Bonhoeffer," said the young man and he set about finding a pan to heat the lunch.

"He's the only one I allow in here," said Mrs. Bonhoeffer. "That's because he cleans the place." She beckoned Ella to her side. "And," she added *sotto voce*, "He's a prince of a guy!" The two withdrew past the kitchen counter to the dining hall. In a hushed voice Mrs.Bonhoeffer continued, "I've been watching you. Somehow you are special. I think both of you can do better than mac and cheese for lunch. Go to the store. I'll give you a list: a pepper, some sausage, tomato sauce and paste, some kale and a small package of vermicelli." She gave Ella an up and down appraisal. "I've been observing you, and I think you and I can come up with an especially fine sauce for real spaghetti! That will be far better than mac and cheese, better for both of you! Let me get my purse; I'll give you the money."

"Oh, no," said Ella as she pulled the twenty out of her pocket. "It's kind of you, but I have enough."

Ella's spaghetti and its delicious sauce were a hit with the young man, as was Ella, who in turn was smitten with him. Ella sensed the periodic discreet presence of Mrs. Bonhoeffer in the hallway, checking perhaps on the progress of her bit of match-making.

Just like a fairy godmother, thought Ella.

Ella and the young man did get married, of course, and set about living happily ever after. Ella's stepmother came to the wedding, parading grandly to the front pew, escorted by Ella's father, who devoted his attention to his cell phone and uttered occasional growls during the service as his team was in the process of losing again. Ella generously included both Detroit and Atlanta in her wedding party, although they couldn't agree about who would process up the aisle first and insisted on walking side by side instead of one behind the other. The man in the white dress conducted the ceremony in which Ella insisted there be no promise to "obey".

Over time Ella taught the young man a great deal about how to clean almost anything. He soon grew his church kitchen floor mopping to become the owner of the largest janitorial service in the five county area. Ella joined the church and found herself working side by side with

Mrs. Bonhoeffer, eventually succeeding her to become the ruler of the kitchen. She allowed everyone in the kitchen who wanted to be there.

"It's not a problem," she explained. "I don't mind a bit if they make a mess. I've done a lot of kitchen cleaning in my time!"

Ella finally found out the meaning of *begat* so she and the young man had three children: two boys and a girl. The boys enjoyed being with their mother in the kitchen and they soon mastered the Ella/Bonhoeffer recipe for superb spaghetti sauce. The girl didn't care much for the kitchen and spent little time there. She figured she'd grow up to have servants.

Hansel and Gertie

Another Mangled Fairy Tale

Standing lost and bewildered amid acres of pine trees that would be someone's well-funded retirement when they were harvested, Hansel and Gertie were trying to figure out their next move.

"If I could get reception, we'd easily see how to get out of here," said Hansel.

"I told you, you should have asked directions before we started into the woods," said Gertie to her brother. "Typical male. I had to have been born with a brother, of course."

"This thing works fine out in the open—except for the voice," said Hansel. "When she says 'End of messages', it sounds like she's saying 'End of Methodists'".

"I wish you'd have dropped bread crumbs like Hansel in the story," said Gertie. "Then we could have seen our way back to where we started."

"We'd have been fine if it weren't for the sea gulls following us."

"There wouldn't have been sea gulls if you hadn't been dropping red herrings all along the way. Bread crumbs would have been better."

"Then it would have been blue jays. Same result."

Hansel turned slowly in a circle. "Moss grows on the north side of a tree and the sun tracks along the south from east to west," he said.

"That's fine, except there's no moss on any of the trees here and these woods are so thick we can't see the sun."

"If you'd quiet down, I could think of something," said Hansel.

"Think all you want; I'm going this way," said Gertie, and off she headed along a path between the trees made by passing deer.

Hansel ran to catch up.

They walked until they thought they couldn't walk another step. One more step took them into a clearing, however, and there they saw it: their mother's house.

It was a cottage all gingerbreaded-up with ornate scrollwork along the eaves and at the peak of the roof, fancy trim around the front door, intricate carving in the window shutters, multi-paned windows with planter boxes beneath them, and flowering shrubs and bulbs in beds along the house foundations. The deer path led straight to several bird feeders.

Brother and sister walked right into the house via the front door.

"Hi, Mom; we're home!" they said together, as if they'd rehearsed their chorus for days.

"Oh, dearies, it's so good to see you!" said Mother, who wore a hot pink silk dressing gown and stiletto high heels. She had been sitting in her cane rocking chair, but rose to greet the twins. Teetering on her high heels, Mother towered above them and bent down to give them each a hug. She's still drop-dead gorgeous, thought Gertie. It's the same perfume I remember, thought Hansel.

"Hansel, I'll need to re-arrange your room," said Mother. "Your room became my sewing and hobby room when you left for college, so you'll have to couch-surf until things get straightened out. And Gertie, your room is just as it was when you left. Sentimental me, I haven't had the heart to change a thing."

The duo followed Mother down a hall. Mother opened a door and gestured to Gertie. "See," she said.

"Mom! It's a mess!"

"I told you," said Mother. She picked up her phone. "What do you want on your pizza?" she asked. "And while we have dinner, you can tell me all about your plans, now that you have your degrees. You can tell me about your job offers and where you'll be living and how much you'll be earning. You can just tell me everything!"

Hansel and Gertie looked at each other.

"Um, sure!" they said together.

*   *   *   *   *   *   *   *   *   *

*

"I don't need to measure your finger to know you're just sitting around here getting fat," said Mother to Hansel. "If at least you were looking for a job it would be a lot better! Besides, you two just hanging around here like parasites cramps my style."

"Mom, jobs are hard to find just now," said Hansel. "There isn't much out there for Art History majors, at least around here."

"Well, then, there are things you can be doing around here to earn your keep. The grass needs mowing. And while you're out there, take the big clippers to that hedge. It's grown so thick that even a prince with a sword couldn't cut through it!"

"So, maybe Sleeping Beauty could do something, too?"

"Your sister needs all the beauty sleep she can get," said

Mother. "But she'll have chores soon enough. And I don't want you

sneaking any more of my chocolate bon-bons. They're mine and I need

them as chasers for my champagne. When you get that job, you can buy

your own! Now, scoot; I need to set up my tennis date."

Hansel shuffled outside. "Don't worry, be happy," he told

himself. "Whoever thought up whistling while working must have been

a brick short." In the garage, which was the cottage's former stable, he

found the big clippers. The grass could wait, he thought. It would be

best to start on the thick hedge while he had fresh energy.

The hedge was very thick and as Hansel hacked an opening

further and further into it, the thick hedge made his path darker and

darker. After some time, he had to stop for rest. There was a stump to

sit on, which Hansel thought was handy enough and convenient.

"Careful where you're putting the lard!" said an alarmed voice.

Hansel looked around and could see nothing.

"You almost squashed me," said the voice.

Hansel looked down. There, half-hidden in the leaves was a

green frog.

"You can talk?" said Hansel.

"Obviously," replied the frog.

"I didn't know toads could talk."

"I'm a frog, not a toad." The frog paused. "Actually, that's not the truth. I'm really a princess."

Hansel thought a moment. "This is a little upside down," he said.

"Oh, you're right," said the frog. "In fact, before I became a frog, I was a bear for a year."

"So if I kiss you, as in the fairy tale, you'll turn into a beautiful princess?"

"I don't know for sure. I could turn into a princess. Or a bear. Or a handsome prince. Who can tell?"

"How about if I just pet you, then?" said Hansel.

"How about if you take me home instead?"

"We'll need a terrarium and I don't think Mom has one."

"Then put me in a box in a corner of your room."

"I don't have a room—at least not yet. I'm couch surfing until Mother cleans out my room and I get it back."

"I've been watching. You've been home for months now and she spends most of her time having coffee with friends or playing tennis at the club. She likes cocktails early. Since she hasn't gotten around to your room, a corner of it should be safe for some time. And over time you could grow to like me, maybe even love me, and then you'd kiss me."

"But what if you're a handsome prince or even a bear? What then?" asked Hansel.

"No relationship has its guarantees," said the frog. "You take what you get. Besides, there's always couples counseling."

Hansel thought. Thinking was hard work. Finally, he bent down and picked up the frog. "Into my pocket you go!" he said.

*   *   *   *   *   *   *   *   *   *

When Hansel and the frog returned to the cottage, they found Gertie cleaning ashes from the woodstove. Soot smeared her face and her sweatshirt was flecked with ash.

"Look what I found!" Hansel said to his sister.

"Oh, a toad!"

"No, silly; it's a frog!" said Hansel. "At least right now it's a frog."

"Mother will never allow a frog in the house," said Gertie. "Remember when you had those ring-necked snakes and they all got loose? Mom really freaked out."

"This is different. Snakes don't like to be petted—or kissed."

"Yes, kissed!" said the frog.

"A talking frog?" said Gertie.

"What do you think? You heard it. I'm not a ventriloquist. So, where's Mom?"

"Out."

"Out, where?"

"I don't know. She took your GPS, so she could be anywhere and unable to find her way back."

"I need to find a place for my little friend," said Hansel.

"Toadying already?" said Gertie.

"That's not funny!' said Hansel. "What do you think about a roasting pan?"

"That might work."

"Terrible idea," said the frog.

"It really does talk!" exclaimed Gertie.

"And?"

"I'll get the roasting pan. Let's do it now, before Mother gets home."

"Forget the cover," said the frog. "I need light."

Gertie disappeared into the kitchen and returned promptly with a blue oblong roasting pan. "Won't you need some grass or leaves or something?" she asked.

"You're sweet," said the frog. "And besides, you're really very pretty."

Gertie blushed. She never heard compliments like that from her brother. She flicked back a strand of hair by her ear, leaving a smear of ashes along the side of her face.

"You're sweet, too," Gertie told the frog. "Why, for that I could just give you a nice kiss and hug!"

"What on earth are you thinking?" said Mother, who teetered behind them on platform tennis shoes.

"We were just. . . . " Hansel and Gertie said together.

"We were just being nice," said the frog.

Mother's jaw dropped in amazement.

"A talking toad!" she said.

"I'm a frog."

"Ah, I get you. And just like in the fairy tales, if someone kisses you, then you turn into a handsome prince."

The frog remained silent. Hansel and Gertie looked at each other.

"Well, I certainly could use a handsome prince around here," said Mother. "At least there would be a fortune involved—which beats two people with college degrees and no jobs."

"Mother, you know we've tried," chorused Hansel and Gertie together.

Mother reached and grabbed the frog from Hansel's hand. She held it at arm's length and then, in a sudden but smooth motion, brought the frog to her lips and kissed it. As mother turned into a pumpkin, the frog dropped to the floor.

"Oh, dear," it said. "I'm still a frog.

"But maybe you're a handsome prince or a beautiful princess—or even a bear," chorused Hansel and Gertie.

"Try me and see."

Hansel and Gertie looked at each other. "We'll need to think this through," said Hansel.

"If I kiss you and get a beautiful princess, that would be fine," he said. "But if I kiss you and I get a handsome prince, what then?"

"I wouldn't mind that," said Gertie. "And if I kiss you and I get a vicious bear, what then?"

No one said anything. Hansel was thinking. Again, he found it to be hard work.

"So what are you guys going to do with a pumpkin?" asked the frog.

"There was supposed to be a big dance tonight at the tennis club," said Gertie. "But they changed it to a potluck. We could bring the pumpkin."

"Yes," said Hansel. "Mother always liked the tennis club. She spent a lot of time there."

"One of you will need a dancing partner," said the frog.

"They changed it to a potluck," said Gertie. "And I just don't know what to wear."

"Wear the coveralls," said Hansel. "You wore them all through college. They're just right for a potluck."

"Do you think I should wear my tongue pearl?" asked Gertie.

"No," said Hansel. "When you talk with that thing in, you sound like the voice on my phone: 'End of Methodists'."

Gertie flitted off to her room to change. "You'll need to wash your face," called Hansel.

"Coveralls are so common," said the frog. "Everyone wears them. It's amazing how universal they are among young people striving to express their individuality."

Hansel ignored the frog and looked around for his phone. Finding it, he thought about someone he could text. He thought and thought, but the people that came to mind were the kind of people who bragged on Facebook, so that by the time you finished a session everyone else seemed to be outrageously successful and, by comparison, you were a failure.

Presently, a washed and showered Gertie reappeared in neatly pressed coveralls.

"You clean up well," said the frog.

Gertie blushed. "Do we take the pumpkin?" she asked.

"Sure," said Hansel. "It's a potluck. We'll figure out what to do with it when we get there."

*   *   *

*

As the threesome entered the tennis club's banquet room, they were greeted with a smile by the woman at the desk. "Oh, you brought a pumpkin!" she said. "It's a big one! We'll add it to the door prizes." And she took the pumpkin and put it in a box underneath the table.

Before long, Gertie found herself with a tray standing in front of five large bowls of jello. As she was trying to decide between green jello with pear slices or orange jello with mandarin orange slices, her

tray was jostled by a tall young man with a tray full of salad bowls.
"Excuse me," he said, "but the red jello with apple slices is the best.
Besides, it has the most artistic whipped cream decoration."

"Jello as artwork?" asked Gertie.

"Well, I don't know much about art, but I know what I like," he
said.

"What was it supposed to be before people took scoops of it?"
asked Gertie.

"Hannibal crossing the Alps. Profound--and very evocative."

"You must know a great deal about art, then, despite what you
say," said Gertie.

The young man blushed. "No, actually I'm a hedge fund
manager," he said. "But art's something I'd like to know more about. I
manage a lot of money, so I just don't have time to go to school to learn
about art."

"What you need, then, is a private tutor," said Gertie. "I think I
know someone who might be able to help you with that." The two took
their trays to the far corner of the banquet room and quickly enough
were in deep and close conversation.

Meanwhile, Hansel had been trying to balance his tray and
spear another meatball, but since he had gone vertical, all the items on

his tray were tilting precariously and threatening to slide smoothly off into the punch bowl.

"Here, let me help you," said a melodious female voice. Reaching around Hansel from behind, the voice's braceleted arm deftly deposited the reluctant meatball onto Hansel's full plate.

"Thank you," said Hansel, as he twisted around to see the possessor of the voice. What he saw, he liked. "You did that well," he said. "Do you work here?"

The girl laughed, flashing perfect teeth and a delicate dimple. "No," she said. "I'm a petroleum engineer. I came tonight to get away from the office; I needed a break."

"I'm not sure what a petroleum engineer does," said Hansel. "You have an office somewhere?"

"I do have an office somewhere. I own the building."

"Then you work for a big company?" said Hansel.

"It is a big company. I own it."

"Wow! An oil company and an office building!" said Hansel, truly impressed.

"And you?" said the girl. "You're a member here? I haven't seen you before."

"No, actually my mother has the membership here. My sister and I came because we needed a break and Mother really doesn't cook. And tonight, especially, she couldn't cook."

"Did she injure herself?"

"Well, not exactly," said Hansel. "She's just not herself tonight. She was feeling a little strange."

"That's too bad. I'm sorry to hear that," said the girl. "But you must own a company or something or perhaps you're a consultant?"

"Well, no. I'm fresh out of college. Art History."

"Really?" said the girl. "I've been looking for someone to advise the company on finding good artwork for our building. Perhaps you might have some ideas?"

"I might, " said Hansel.

The two adjourned to discuss the matter. Hansel's vertically piled food tray went uneaten.

Presently, the woman who'd been at the reception desk took the microphone to announce the door prize winners. The first winner got tickets to the high school drama class' new play. The second winner received an over-sized Thermos. "And our third winner is our top Senior Tennis Champion, a man everyone knows," announced the woman. "Stanley Miller, come get your HUGE pumpkin!"

Stanley, a lithe but vertically challenged man with a monk's hairline, bounded to the front to the cheers of everyone in the room.

"Just what I always wanted: a big pumpkin!" he said, as he hoisted it aloft. The room erupted in laughter and cheers. Bringing it down to face level, he gave the pumpkin he was hugging a big kiss.

And there was Mother.

The room went absolutely silent.

Mother bent down to Stanley's height.

"We could play doubles," she said.

*　　　　　　*　　　　　　*

But, you ask, whatever happened to the frog? The frog got a job at the tennis club controlling flies in the kitchen. It was a guest at Hansel's, Gertie's and Mother and Stanley's weddings, all held at the tennis club, of course. In the kitchen, fortunately because the chef was not much into French culinary arts, he and the frog had deep and serious philosophical conversations about how to make good gravy. And because the frog could enjoy the fruits of its labor as a Fly

Elimination Specialist, it considered its compensation package to be quite good, indeed.

Snow Job and the Four Dwarfs

Another Mangled Fairy Tale

by

Mark Hayes Peacock

Three of the seven dwarfs had decided to seek greener pastures. The first dwarf, who was broad-minded and never condescended nor looked down on anyone, became a Peace Corps Volunteer working with Pygmies in Gabon, Central Africa. Things really began to look up for the second dwarf when he became an assistant manager with a National Basketball Association team. The third dwarf enlisted in the military and found duty in Guantanamo reading poetry for four hours daily to an impeached former President of the United States.

That left four dwarfs, who were quite happy around a card table playing everything from poker to Old Maid. Where seven dwarfs would make things too cozy, just four dwarfs almost filled a booth at the local coffee shop where they would gather with other geezers to complain and declaim about how the world was going to hell in a hand basket.

Today, however, the topic was the local prince, who'd been off in the woods using his silver sword to hack his way through acres of brambles, vines and thickets.

"Reminds me of the little kid who was digging through a large pile of horse manure," said the first dwarf. "He figured that with all that horse dung there had to be a pony in there somewhere!"

But it wasn't a pony the young prince sought. He figured that with so much growth to hack through there had to be a princess at the end of his quest. *And when I find her,* he thought, *the first thing I'll do is to take up this mess with the Forestry Service and the Bureau of Land Management. It's a gigantic fire hazard; the whole thing could erupt in a holocaust and cause all sorts of damage! I'll talk with them as soon as the government ends its shutdown and there's someone's around I can talk with.*

And so the prince hacked away, swinging his silver sword right and left, stopping to rest occasionally and looking back to see how far he had come. It was slow going.

At last his sword broke through the undergrowth and he found himself in a clearing. There was a decrepit hut in the clearing with moss on its roof shingles, spider webs hanging from its soffits, windows in need of caulk, and a bucket of water by the door for the animals that had been watching the prince's slow progress through the forest's thickets.

And there in the clearing on her back with her eyes closed, lying on a bed of willow branches padded with moss, lay the most gorgeous creature the prince had ever seen. She wore a sky blue gown with a plunging neckline and had a gold belt around an impossibly narrow waist. Her feet boasted black patent leather slippers. Her dark hair framed a heart-shaped face of ivory skin and her eyelashes were so long that when they were batted they could have created a draft in even a very large room. Her ruby lips invited discovery.

The prince sheathed his sword and circled the beautiful maiden. He figured she had to be a princess; no one else could have boasted the physical qualities he saw in front of him. His quest had not been in vain.

But now what? He touched her shoulder. No response. His princess still slept. Gently, he shook her shoulder. Still, no response. *If I tickle her feet?* he thought but wiggled her foot instead. No response. The princess still slept. "Hello?" he said. Nothing. "Hello!" he said in a louder voice. Nothing.

Then it dawned on him: what was needed was a kiss, just like in the fairy tales his mother read to him when he was a child. *This will be easy,* he thought as he bent over her somnolent form. But as he lowered his face to hers the hilt of his sword jabbed him in the ribs.

"Damn, I forgot!" he said aloud. "These days you have to ask permission."

But how to ask when the recipient of a future kiss was so fast asleep that she couldn't assent? Nothing the prince had done so far had caused the princess even to stir. Casting around him, the prince thought there might be something that would make a very loud noise so his princess would awake. He found nothing.

But then he saw the water bucket. He strode to the shack door, picked up the wildlife's water bucket and brought it to the princess' bedside. He dumped the entire bucket full on her head.

In addition to waking up the sleeping princess, the water swept her eyelashes to the ground. Pale skin dribbled into her dark hair and down onto the bed. Those ruby lips remained but now against her skin the botox job was obvious.

"Who are you and what the hell do you think you're doing?" she demanded.

"I was just trying to wake you up," he responded, more than a bit startled.

"You did a great job!" she said. "And what was your need to wake me up, may I ask?"

"Well, that's how it's supposed to turn out," he said. "Besides, I worked hard for weeks just to get here and to find you!"

Warily, she eyed the prince. "Are you delivering a subpoena?" she asked.

"A what?"

"A subpoena? Are you one of those process servers—or whatever they call you?"

The prince laughed. "No," he said with great charm. "I am a prince with a kingdom to inherit and I'm in need of a princess to go with it. And now I've found you."

"What a con," she said. "Kingdoms. Princes. Princesses. All those are relics of the past. I don't believe a word of it!"

"But it's true! I really am a prince. Look, I'll prove it: here's my singing sword."

He took his sword from its scabbard and handed it to her.

"It's dull," she said.

"Of course it's dull; I've been hacking away with it for weeks now just to get to you, so of course it's dull."

"Show me an I.D."

The prince looked perplexed. Tunics and tights have no pockets and princes have no wallets. They always borrow what they need from their servants, footmen or butlers.

He took back his sword. "I can't show you an I.D." he said. "I don't need one. Everyone in the kingdom knows me so all I have to do is wave back."

She gave the prince a once up and down. He did look like he could be a prince. "Let's go in the house," she said. "I need a mirror."

"Why don't we go to your castle?" he proposed.

"There is no castle. This is my refuge, my getaway."

Flummoxed, the prince trailed her into the miserable hut.

She found a mirror and stood aghast. "Look what you've done!" she said.

The prince didn't know what to say. "I need to do some repair work!" declared his princess and she disappeared through a heavy and creaking wooden door.

"You're new around here?" croaked a voice from the shadows on the far side of the room. In the dim light the prince could make out a small form. As it began to move into the light the prince saw an old crone that continued to speak.

"She's right about no castle," said the crone. "She's no princess, either. But this is her getaway, just as she said. Here, she can be treated as if she were a princess. For that matter—and as a young man it's good for you to know this—every woman at heart wants to be treated like a princess."

"So this is like some sort of spa?"

"You could say that. Here, she gets the royal treatment: massage, sunbathing, a chance to get out of those pantsuits and to dress up, eat organic food and to escape from fluorescent lighting and a corner office.

"She didn't have a chance to tell you. She's the owner and CEO of the major gold mining company in this area. Her days are spent meeting with legislators and regulators and environmental groups and even with the miners. Lots of pressure; that's why she takes a break here."

"And you?"

The crone shrugged. "I'm just here." Then, changing the subject back to the not-princess, she continued, "As I said, she deals with a lot."

"And they're all ungrateful!" declared the princess, who returned to the room after managing to re-install her false eyelashes and re-make her face. "A bunch of ignoramuses, especially those environmentalists. As for the miners, they're a bunch of ingrates! I talk until I'm blue in the face about the benefits I bring to everyone: jobs! I'll say it again: jobs! For every dollar those lousy miners earn, seven more are generated into the local economy. And, someday, we will go back to the gold standard and everyone around here will be rich. Rich, I say, rich!"

"Who would object to that?" asked the prince.

"Yes, who? Those regulators, politicians and environmentalists don't understand how much better my planned approach will be than the way gold has been mined before. No more tunneling! To do that economically you need narrow tunnels. For narrow tunnels, you need dwarfs. These days, dwarfs are hard to find; they've been a shrinking commodity since 'The Wizard of Oz'!

"So my plan is to change the entire industry of gold mining. Instead of tunneling into the mountain, I'll just level it. And that's Biblical: the prophet Isaiah said 'Every valley shall be filled, and every mountain and hill shall be made low', so even the conservative evangelicals around here ought to be happy about my plan. But no; it has to be a big fight! All I'm asking for are fewer regulations, some tax relief, and to be exempt from the fund to treat gold lung disease. In return, I'll bring jobs, jobs, jobs to this region! Did you hear me? I said JOBS! And if you're really a prince, you ought to have some influence around here."

The prince didn't know quite what to say. Jobs wasn't something he could relate to. "So no more dwarfs?" he asked.

"Ingrates! They all quit and went to town. Without them and with small tunnels, I really need to make those changes I was talking about."

She turned on her heel and left through the same large door, tossing over her shoulder as she went a request for perfumed water whenever the crone could bring it.

"Nap time," observed the crone. She took an apple from a bowl on the table and found a small sharp knife. Carefully, she sliced the apple into equal pieces and put several of them on a plate in a tray intended for the princess. Offering a slice to the prince, she said, "They're organic. Golden Delicious. Try one."

Back in the village the geezers nursed the last of the morning's coffee and watched the four dwarfs enter their limousine as their chauffer held the door open for them. They fit easily into a single back seat.

"They can't be called dwarfs anymore; it's not politically correct," observed the third geezer, a retired professor. "They're 'VC's'."

"VC's? Viet Cong?"

"No, 'Vertically Challenged'."

"Must be nice," said the first geezer. "Gold lung disease. They cough, up comes some gold, they put it in a hankie, take it to the assayer and get cash in return."

"That's how they fund their retirement," said the second geezer. "All because there's gold in them thar hills!"

"They earned it," said a third geezer. "Mining's hard work."

"Beats what you did all those years," said a fourth geezer. "University professor. Tenured, so you couldn't be fired. Got your grad students to do your research so you could write the papers and get all the credit and all those guest speaker fees. I don't mind seeing those little guys come out OK."

The third geezer turned bright red. He snatched the cardboard cylinder from the fourth geezer. "Gimmie those damned dice!" he said, as he tossed them and lost. "Black coffee for your black heart!" he said as he reached for his wallet.

The wallet-less prince thought the crone's apple was quite good and said so. Then, making conversation, he asked, "So, how long have you been an old crone?"

"Ever since I had a big change in my life," she replied. She peered at the prince over the tops of her glasses. "Young man, another thing for you to know is that inside every old woman is the girl she was when she was sixteen. Understand that and they'll all think you are a real prince of a guy!"

She sliced another apple, placed the slices on a plate and held the plate out to the prince. Suddenly realizing his hunger after all that time hacking away at the brambles and thickets, the prince reached for the plate she proffered and missed. The plate dropped to the floor and broke. Quickly, both crone and prince knelt to pick up the fallen apple slices and pieces of the broken dish. Face to face on hands and knees their eyes met. Drawn as if by some magnetic force their faces came closer together and with their kiss the crone instantly transformed into a beautiful young woman with natural long eyelashes, hazel eyes beneath them, smooth ivory skin and lips that invited a repeat meeting of their lips.

"I don't believe it!' said the prince. He stood, extended his hand and helped her to her feet. "What happened to you? How did you ever get that way? Did you have old crone's disease?"

" Sometime I'll tell you," she said with a smile. . "It's a bit like one of those old fairy tales and it has something to do with the Golden Rule. You were being gallant, a gentleman, and so you see the result."

"Are you a real princess then, like in the fairy tales?" asked the prince.

"Only if you make it so," she said.

The prince grinned and said, "I think we could work that out."

About Mark Hayes Peacock

Mark Hayes Peacock sold his first national magazine story in 1971. More than forty years of freelance writing followed for national, regional, and local magazines and newspapers, including contributing editorships, cover stories and monthly columns. After retiring, he began writing fiction, including the six mangled fairy tales in this collection. His two paperback books, *The First Gathering of The Break Time Stories* and *The Second Gathering of The Break Time Stories*, are available through Amazon.com, as are six Kindle story collections: *Four Break Time Stories; More Break Time Stories; Yet More Break Time Stories; Four More Break Time Stories; Yes, More Break Time Stories;* and *Another Four Break Time Stories.*

Mr. Peacock lives and writes in Luck, Wisconsin. His wife, Marina, is a retired mental health therapist. They are parents to a gaggle of highly successful children.